Because of You

By Teisha Pessoa

Illustrations by Ambadi Kumar

Published by One2Mpower Publishing LLC

Illustrations by Ambadi Kumar

Because of YOU

My mom is a Pediatrician. Her name is Dr. Vilma Pessoa and we live in Montgomery, Alabama. My mom is well known in the community because of her hard work and dedication to her patients. She has been an inspiration, especially to the little girls.

Because of YOU, little black girls in Montgomery, Alabama dream BIG, not small, because you were their doctor and took care of them All.

Because of YOU, little black girls knew if they worked hard and stayed in school, they could become a doctor, just like you.

Because of YOU, little black girls did not go to the doctor in fear, because you put them at ease and wiped away their tears.

Because of YOU, little black girls know how looking good feels, because you were the BEST dressed Doctor, from your head to your heels.

Because of YOU, little black girls learned about nutrition, healthy lifestyle choices, and personal care, because having a doctor like you was quite rare.

Because of YOU, little black girls grew up
to be mommies too! When in doubt, you
helped them out, because that is what you
loved to do.

Because of YOU, little black girls were proud

of where they came from, no matter their

address, you were the doctor for everyone.

Because of YOU, little black girls looked forward to getting a treat after their checkup. You always gave them something sweet.

Because of YOU, little black girls will read

this book with such admiration, because you

were more than their doctor, you are TRULY

an inspiration!

Because of YOU, little black girls are great
women today, and after 46 years of service,
you deserve to be honored in every way.

Acknowledgements from the Author to Dr. Vilma Pessoa

I am proud to say that my mom is a great Pediatrician. She performed many different roles, all at once. She is a super hero! She managed her work while tending to my needs. She found balance with her career and family. I always felt her love and presence and despite being busy with work, she still found time to bond with me. That is why she is loved, not just by me but by all of us surrounding her.

I used to hope that she would be granted a day, a week, or even a year break for her good deeds and hard work. She is the type of woman I would like to be when I grow up. I would like to be organized, loving, caring, responsible and goal oriented just like her. I am proud that I have a great mom in Dr. Pessoa. I love her as deep as the sea and as high as the tallest mountains. I would not trade her for anything and would love to keep her forever!

Dr. Vilma Pessoa

Made in the USA
Columbia, SC
17 August 2021